the Grouch and the Lovebug

By Josie Monahan

Illustrated by Mark Sean Wilson

the Grouch and the Lovebug

By Josie Monahan

Illustrated by Mark Sean Wilson

INKWELL PRODUCTIONS®
™
The New Face of Publishing

ISBN: 978-1-939625-55-7
Library of Congress Control Number: 2014906421

Published by Inkwell Productions
10869 N. Scottsdale Road # 103-128
Scottsdale, AZ 85254-5280

Tel. 480-315-3781
E-mail info@inkwellproductions.com
Website www.inkwellproductions.com

Printed in the United States of America

Long, long ago in the kingdom
of Cormac lived a king and his
young son, Prince James.

1

2

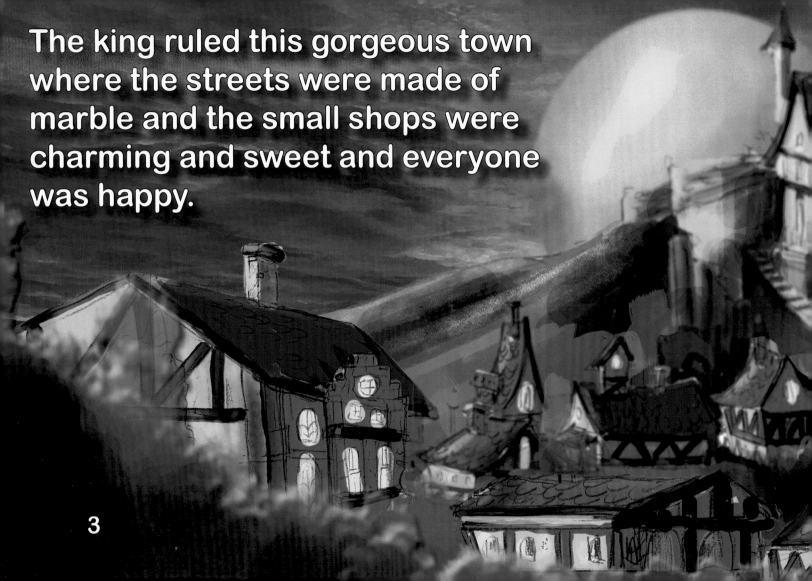

The king ruled this gorgeous town where the streets were made of marble and the small shops were charming and sweet and everyone was happy.

3

4

Prince James was as handsome and kind as his father was rich and powerful. But unfortunately, James had a large scar across his face. And although he kept telling the other children that it was only a birthmark, they made fun of the prince and refused to play with him. Imagine having all the toys in the world and not being able to share them.

5

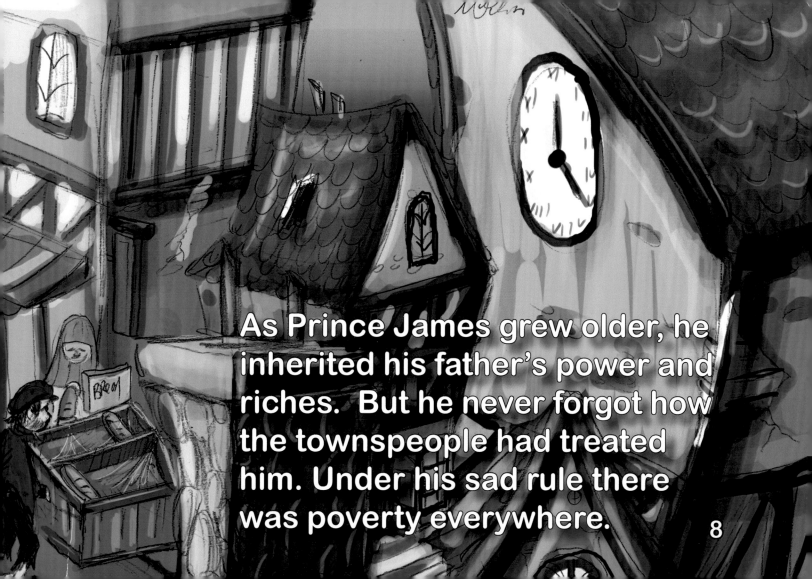

As Prince James grew older, he inherited his father's power and riches. But he never forgot how the townspeople had treated him. Under his sad rule there was poverty everywhere.

8

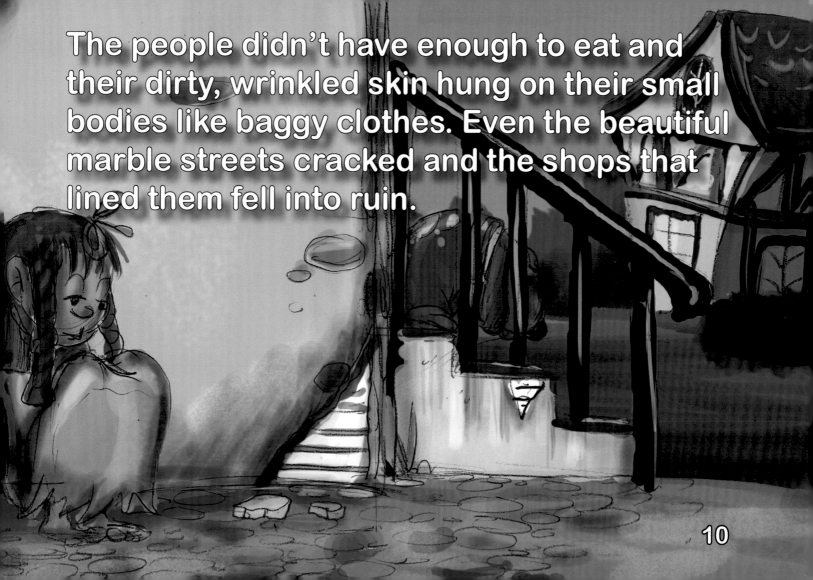

The people didn't have enough to eat and their dirty, wrinkled skin hung on their small bodies like baggy clothes. Even the beautiful marble streets cracked and the shops that lined them fell into ruin.

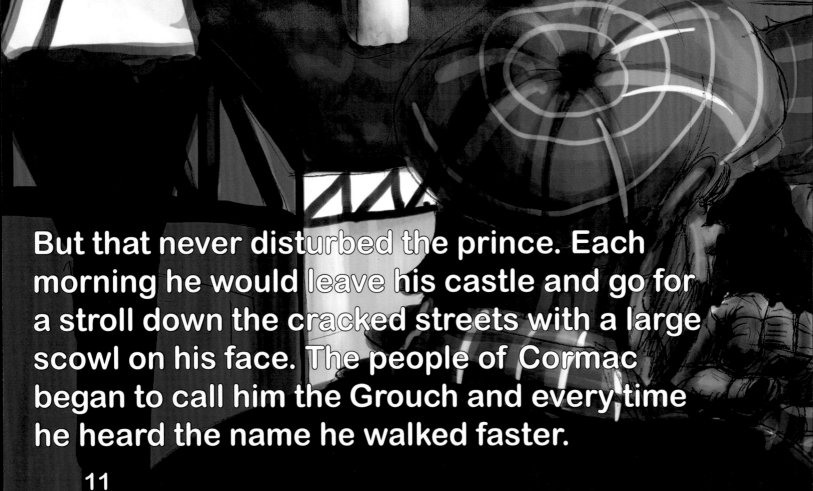

But that never disturbed the prince. Each morning he would leave his castle and go for a stroll down the cracked streets with a large scowl on his face. The people of Cormac began to call him the Grouch and every time he heard the name he walked faster.

12

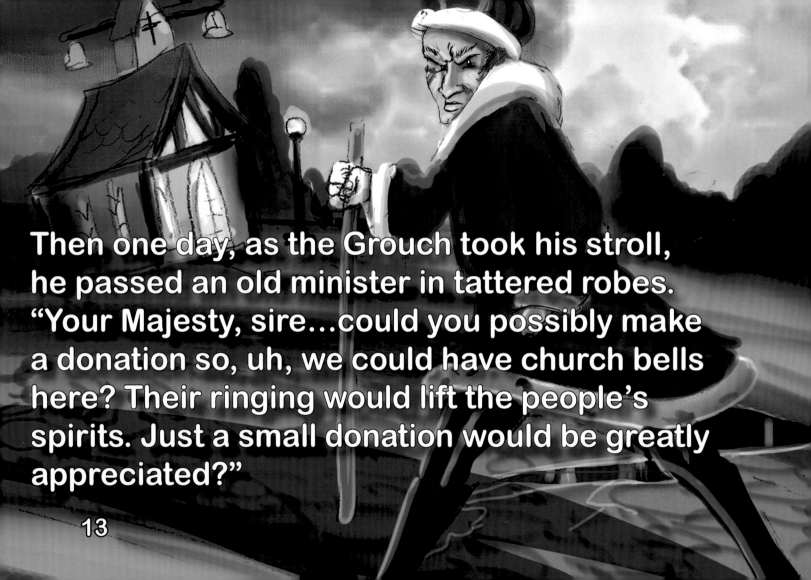

Then one day, as the Grouch took his stroll, he passed an old minister in tattered robes. "Your Majesty, sire…could you possibly make a donation so, uh, we could have church bells here? Their ringing would lift the people's spirits. Just a small donation would be greatly appreciated?"

13

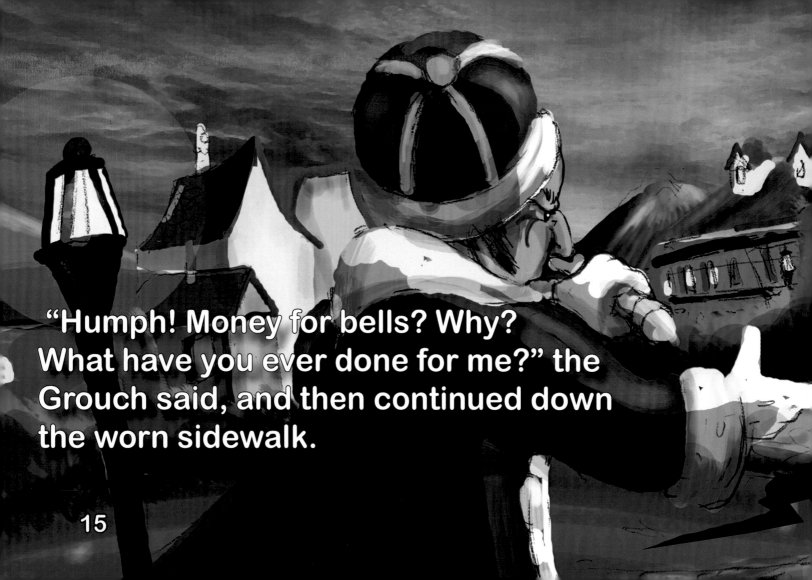

"Humph! Money for bells? Why? What have you ever done for me?" the Grouch said, and then continued down the worn sidewalk.

15

16

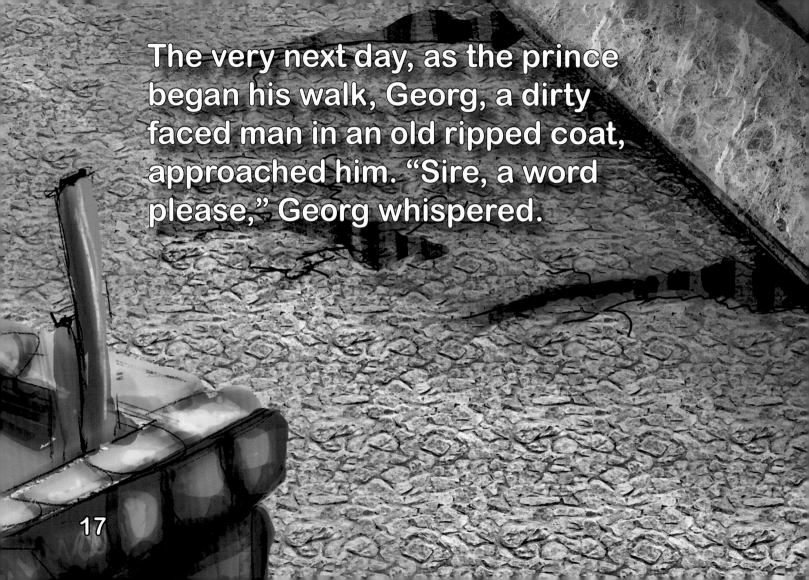

The very next day, as the prince began his walk, Georg, a dirty faced man in an old ripped coat, approached him. "Sire, a word please," Georg whispered.

17

18

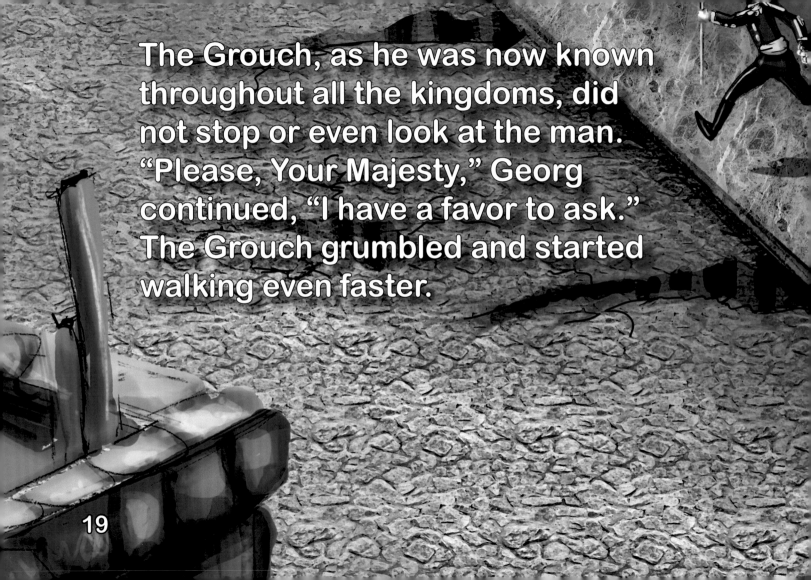

The Grouch, as he was now known throughout all the kingdoms, did not stop or even look at the man. "Please, Your Majesty," Georg continued, "I have a favor to ask." The Grouch grumbled and started walking even faster.

19

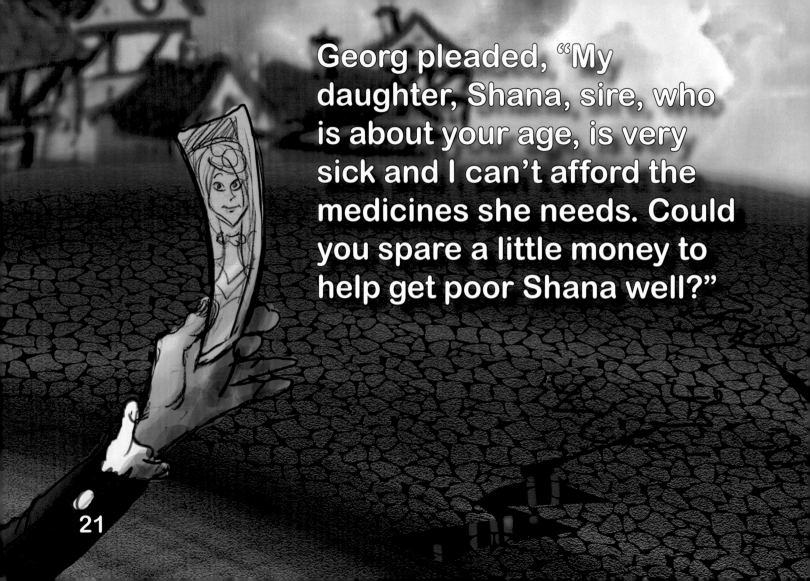

Georg pleaded, "My daughter, Shana, sire, who is about your age, is very sick and I can't afford the medicines she needs. Could you spare a little money to help get poor Shana well?"

21

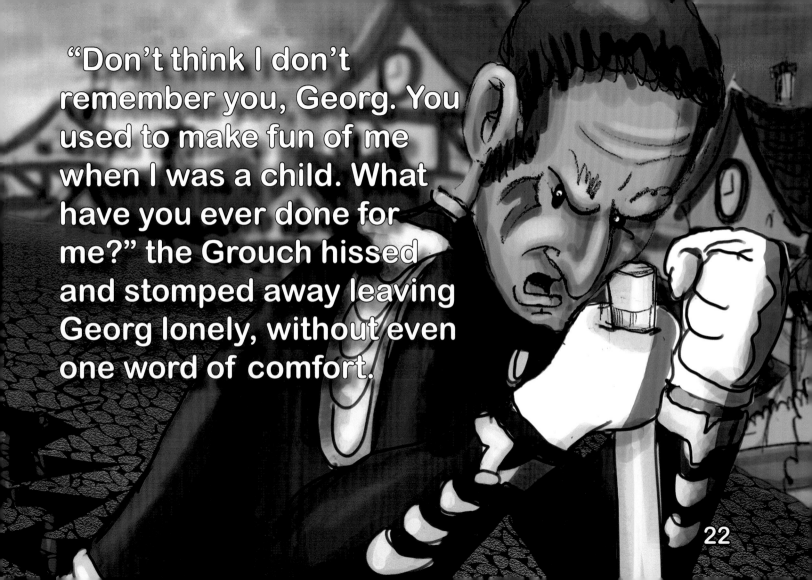

"Don't think I don't remember you, Georg. You used to make fun of me when I was a child. What have you ever done for me?" the Grouch hissed and stomped away leaving Georg lonely, without even one word of comfort.

22

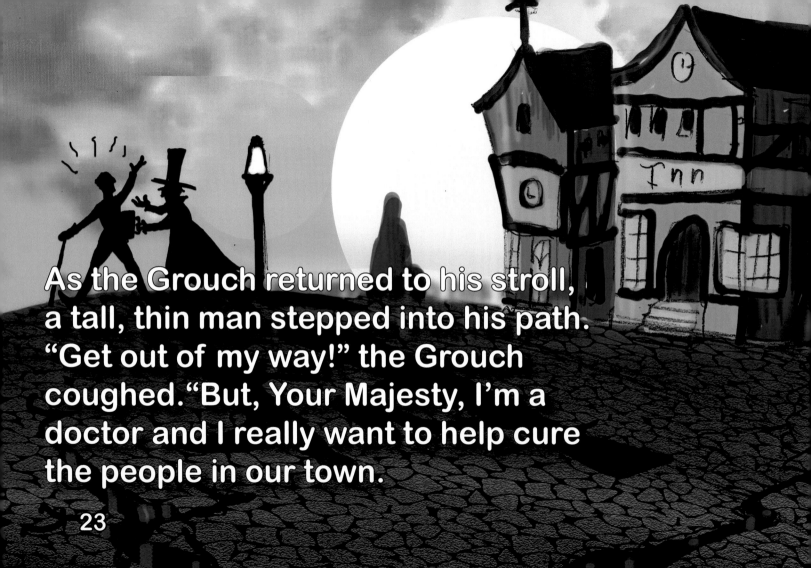

As the Grouch returned to his stroll,
a tall, thin man stepped into his path.
"Get out of my way!" the Grouch
coughed. "But, Your Majesty, I'm a
doctor and I really want to help cure
the people in our town.

23

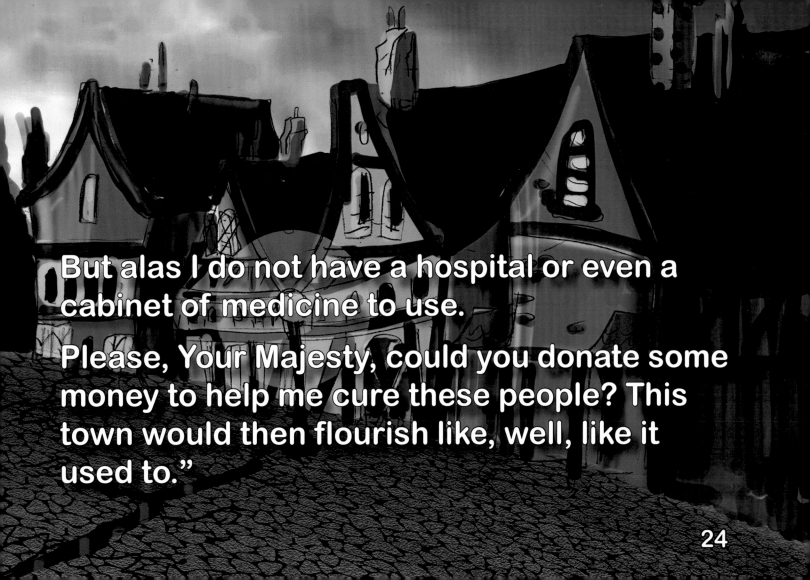

But alas I do not have a hospital or even a cabinet of medicine to use.

Please, Your Majesty, could you donate some money to help me cure these people? This town would then flourish like, well, like it used to."

24

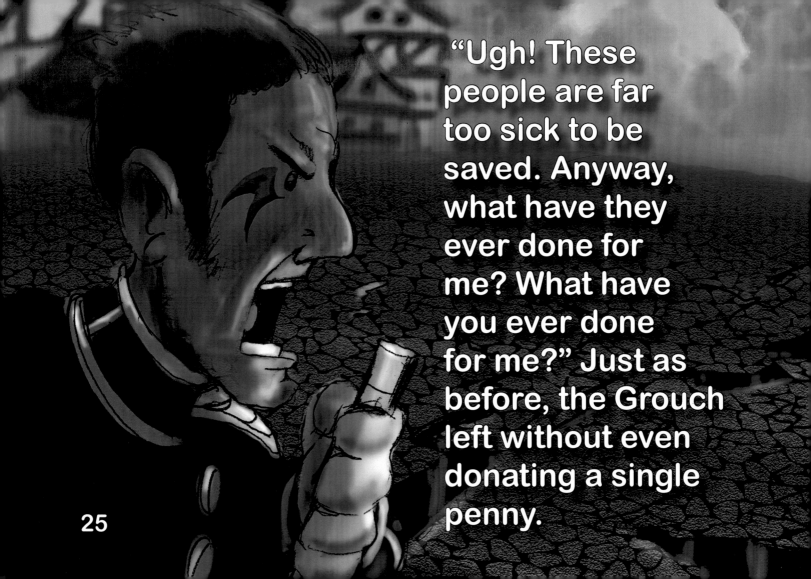

"Ugh! These people are far too sick to be saved. Anyway, what have they ever done for me? What have you ever done for me?" Just as before, the Grouch left without even donating a single penny.

25

A few days later, as the Grouch began his walk, he was not looking where he was going. Suddenly, he tripped over a small pink object lying on the ground. "You." the Grouch grunted. "You're in my way. Move!" He was not in the mood to have his walk interrupted.

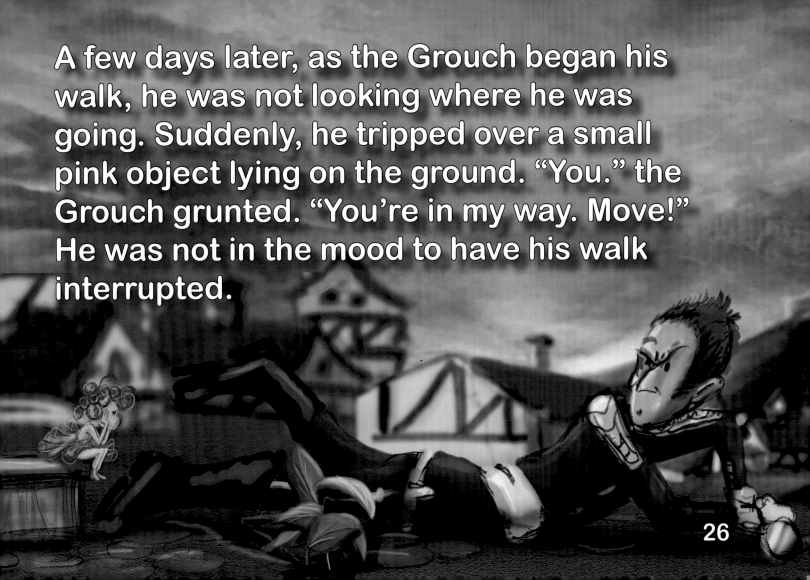

26

"Oh, sir, I'm terribly sad. I have nowhere to live," the little pink figure cried. It looked a bit like a bug but somehow seemed more magical. "You're a bug. Why don't you go live in a tree? There's one over there. Now leave!"

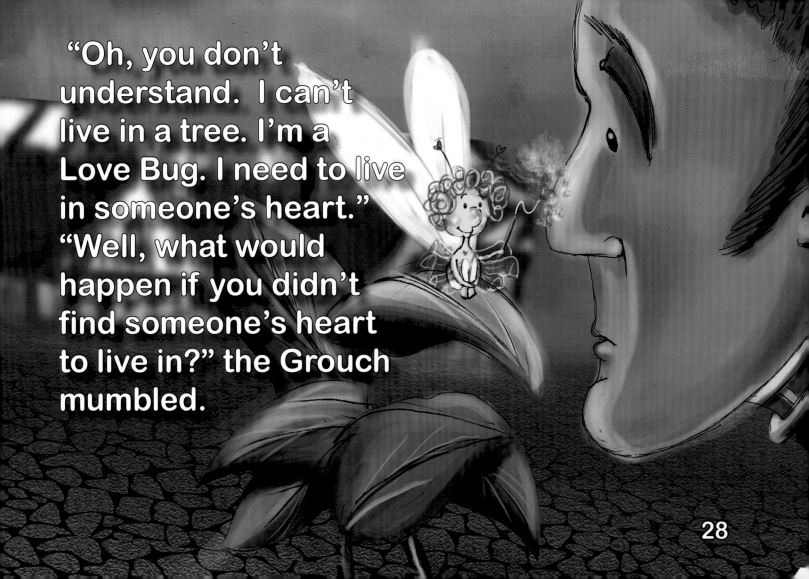

"Oh, you don't understand. I can't live in a tree. I'm a Love Bug. I need to live in someone's heart."

"Well, what would happen if you didn't find someone's heart to live in?" the Grouch mumbled.

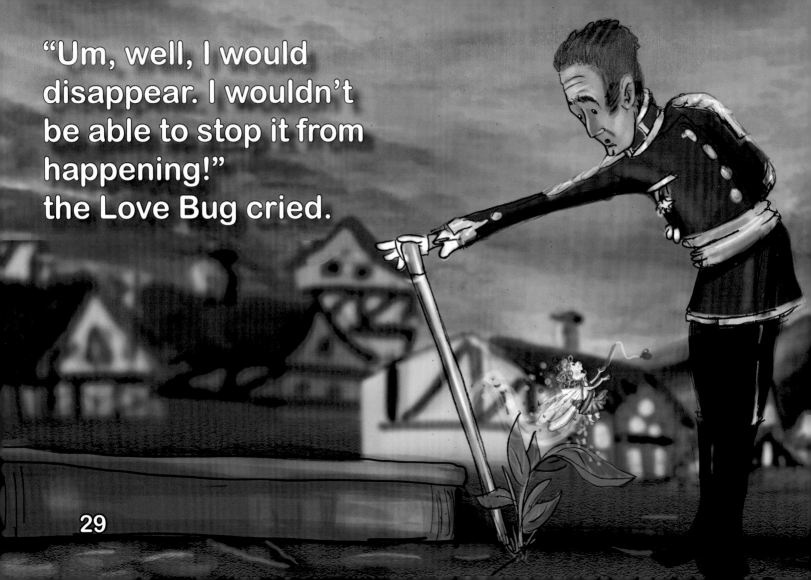

"Um, well, I would disappear. I wouldn't be able to stop it from happening!" the Love Bug cried.

29

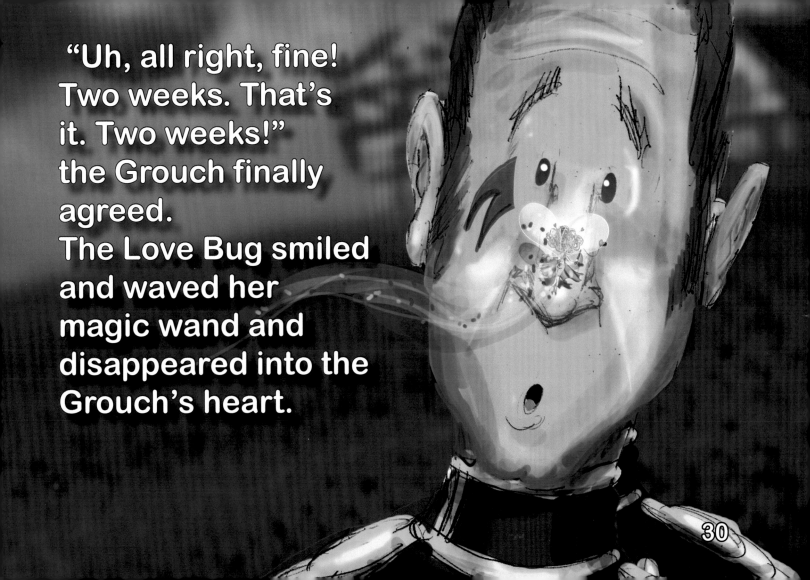

"Uh, all right, fine! Two weeks. That's it. Two weeks!" the Grouch finally agreed. The Love Bug smiled and waved her magic wand and disappeared into the Grouch's heart.

Suddenly the scowl on the Grouch's face melted into a warm smile.

31

But the poor Love Bug was squished because, of course, the Grouch's heart was just a little too small.

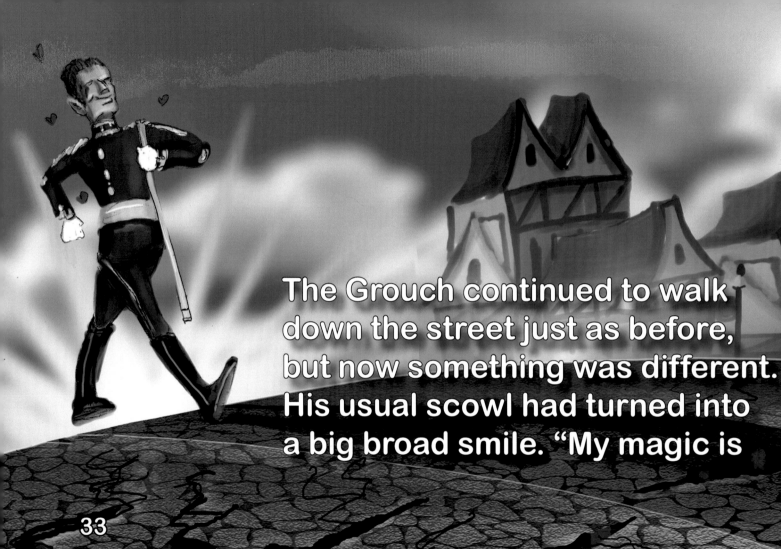

The Grouch continued to walk down the street just as before, but now something was different. His usual scowl had turned into a big broad smile. "My magic is

33

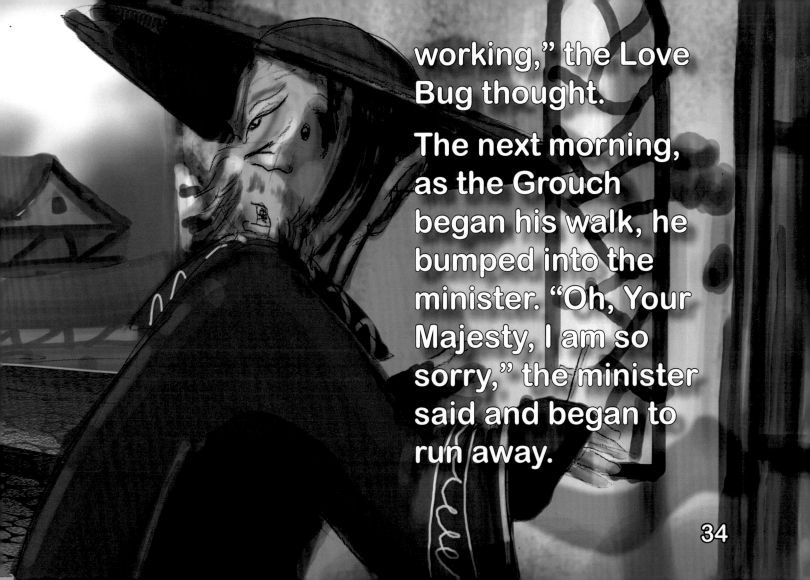

working," the Love Bug thought.

The next morning, as the Grouch began his walk, he bumped into the minister. "Oh, Your Majesty, I am so sorry," the minister said and began to run away.

"No! No! Don't run away. It's all right. Accidents happen. Anyway I wanted to talk to you," the Grouch said and handed the minister a check. "Parson, I want you to go out and buy the biggest most beautiful bells in the whole world."

36

"Oh, sire, are you sure?" the minister said in disbelief. "Sure? I am absolutely sure! And while you're at it, parson, you'd better buy some new clothes too," the Grouch said, smiling.

37

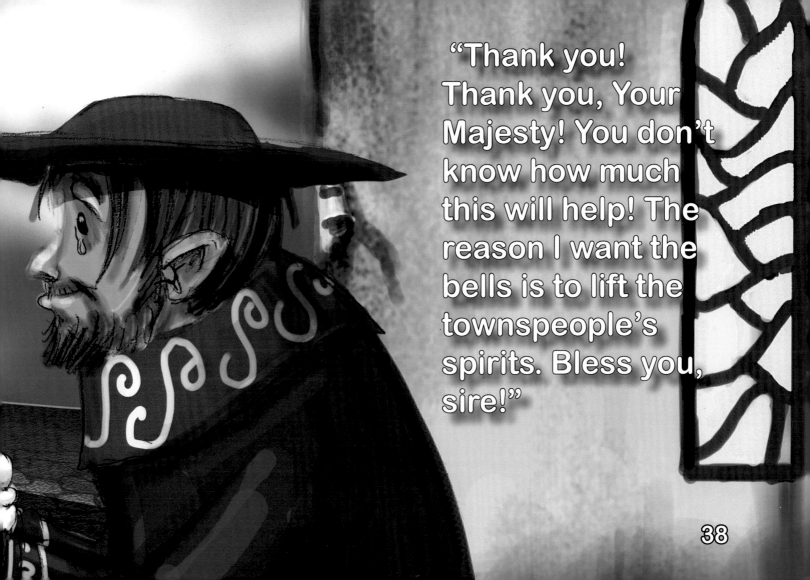

"Thank you! Thank you, Your Majesty! You don't know how much this will help! The reason I want the bells is to lift the townspeople's spirits. Bless you, sire!"

Inside the prince's heart the Love Bug smiled, waved her wand and Prince James' horrible scar began to magically disappear.

39

Later, the Grouch saw Georg sitting down on the street with his head in his hands, crying. "Hello, Georg! I'd like to talk to you!" the Grouch called.

40

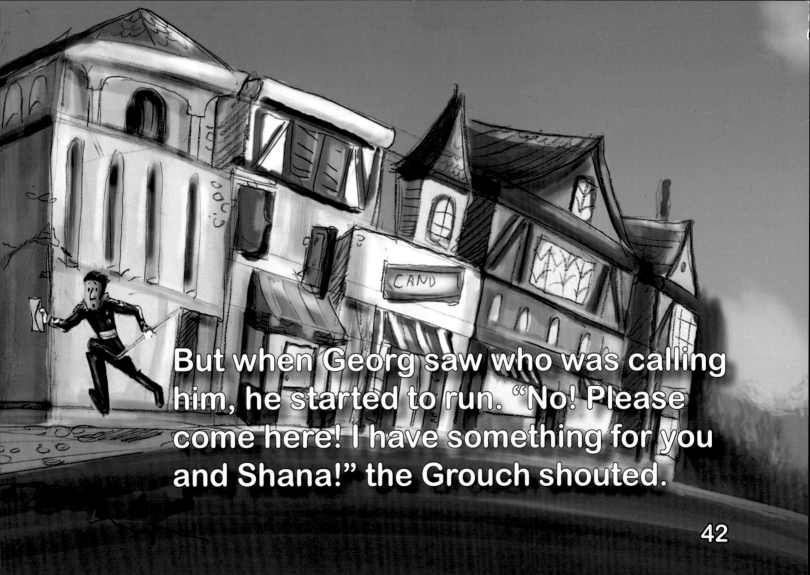

But when Georg saw who was calling him, he started to run. "No! Please come here! I have something for you and Shana!" the Grouch shouted.

"Sire, what do you mean?" Georg asked nervously. "I mean I have something to give you," the Grouch explained and handed Georg an envelope. Inside were bills, lots and lots of bills all lined up perfectly.

" Wh… Why are you giving me money, Your Majesty? What have I ever done for you?" he questioned. "What have you ever done for me?

43

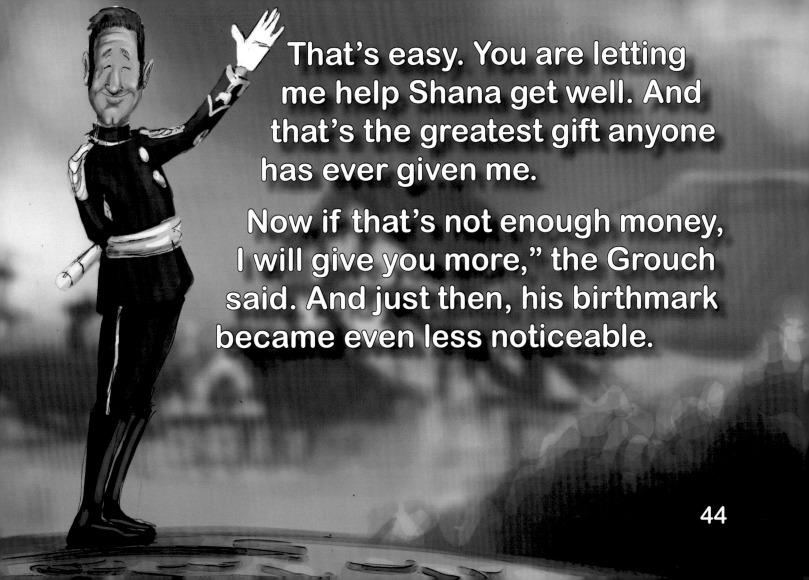

That's easy. You are letting me help Shana get well. And that's the greatest gift anyone has ever given me.

Now if that's not enough money, I will give you more," the Grouch said. And just then, his birthmark became even less noticeable.

44

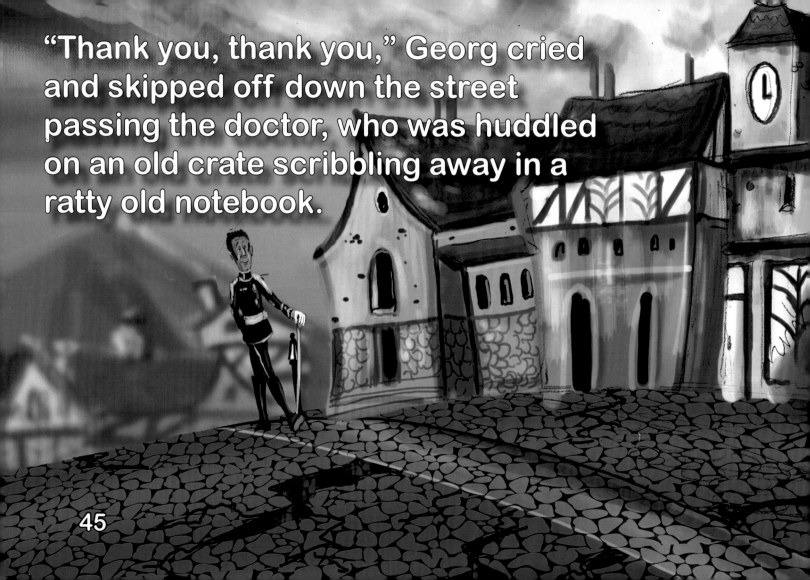

"Thank you, thank you," Georg cried and skipped off down the street passing the doctor, who was huddled on an old crate scribbling away in a ratty old notebook.

46

"Excuse me, doctor, I would like to speak to you." The doctor looked up from his notebook and when he saw who was calling, he hopped up and tried to run away. "Oh, please come back," the Grouch called.

47

"Your Majesty, I'm sorry. Please don't get mad at me. P-p-please?" the doctor pleaded. "Get mad at you? I'll do nothing of the sort. I just wanted to give you this!" the Grouch explained and then handed over a large bag of gold coins. When the doctor saw how much money it was, his eyes bulged out of his face.

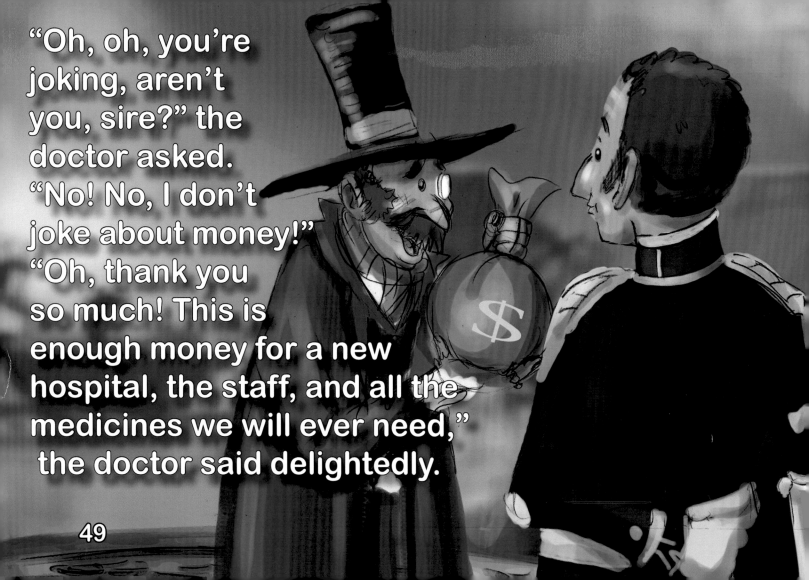

"Oh, oh, you're joking, aren't you, sire?" the doctor asked. "No! No, I don't joke about money!" "Oh, thank you so much! This is enough money for a new hospital, the staff, and all the medicines we will ever need," the doctor said delightedly.

49

"All right, you're welcome. Enjoy your hospital," and the Grouch was off wearing a wide smile on his face. And the Love Bug had an even wider smile as she waved her wand. Suddenly, the prince's scar had disappeared entirely.

50

The prince had never been happier. And no one called him the Grouch anymore. Prince James was aware of that. Then, one day the prince woke up and saw the Love Bug packing her wand in a little suitcase.

52

"Okay, if you say so." The Love Bug shrugged and unpacked her wand, and disappeared into the prince's heart once more. But this time, the Love Bug's home was huge!

HEART ESTATE

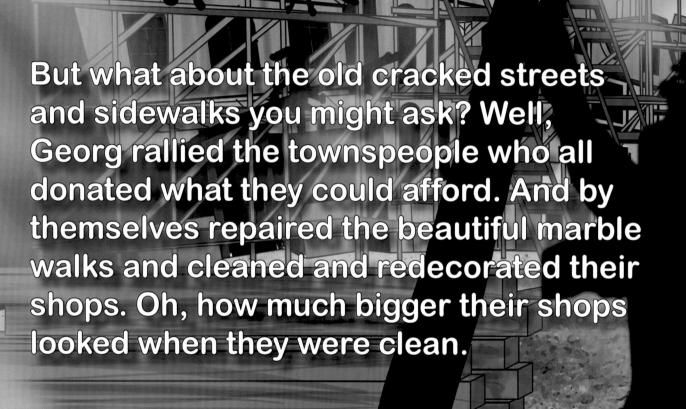

But what about the old cracked streets and sidewalks you might ask? Well, Georg rallied the townspeople who all donated what they could afford. And by themselves repaired the beautiful marble walks and cleaned and redecorated their shops. Oh, how much bigger their shops looked when they were clean.

55

56

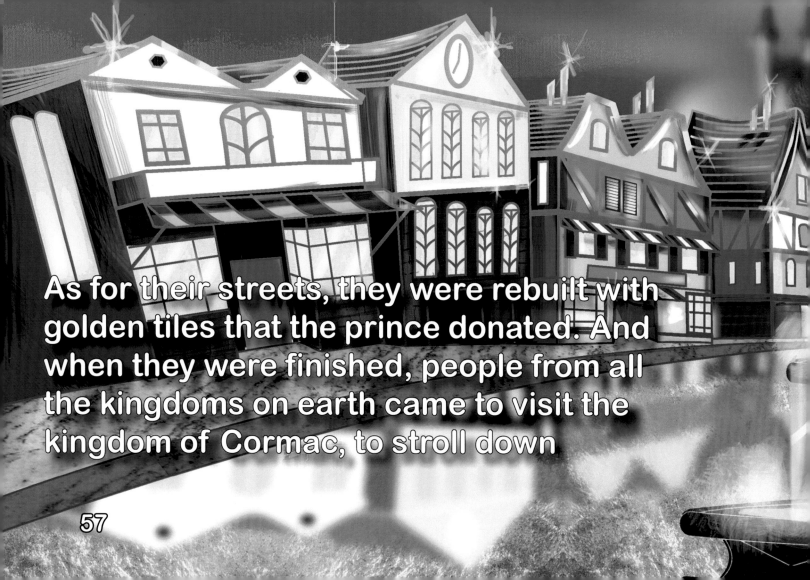

As for their streets, they were rebuilt with golden tiles that the prince donated. And when they were finished, people from all the kingdoms on earth came to visit the kingdom of Cormac, to stroll down

57

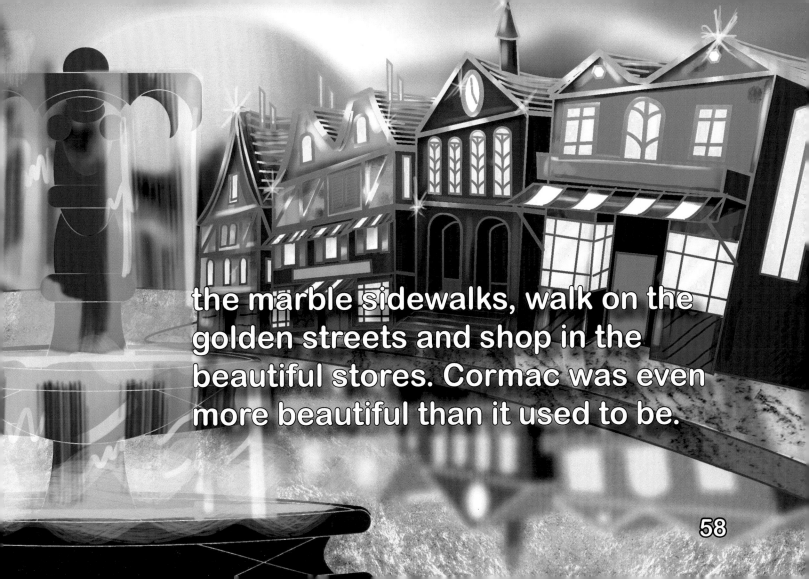

the marble sidewalks, walk on the golden streets and shop in the beautiful stores. Cormac was even more beautiful than it used to be.

EPILOGUE

One day, as Prince James walked down the street, he bumped into Shana by mistake. Oh, but I'm sorry, this meeting was not by mistake. It was, of course, all thanks to the Love Bug and her magic wand.

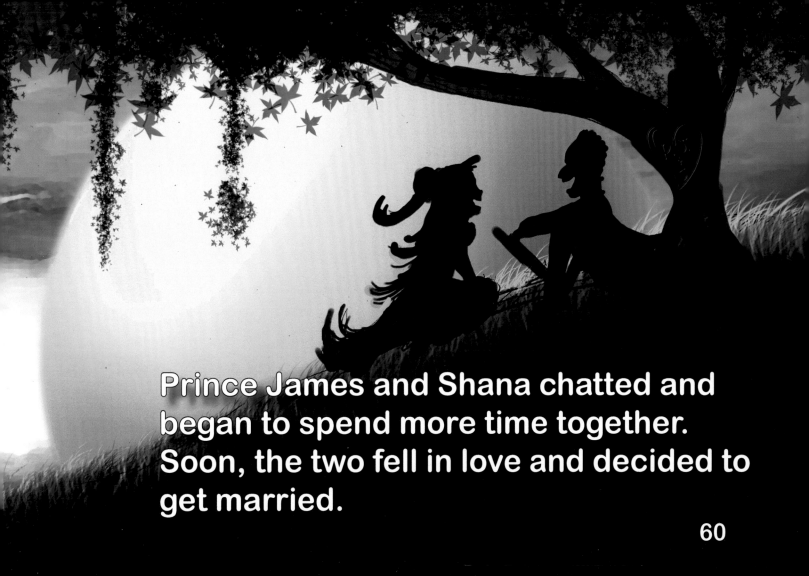

Prince James and Shana chatted and began to spend more time together. Soon, the two fell in love and decided to get married.

60

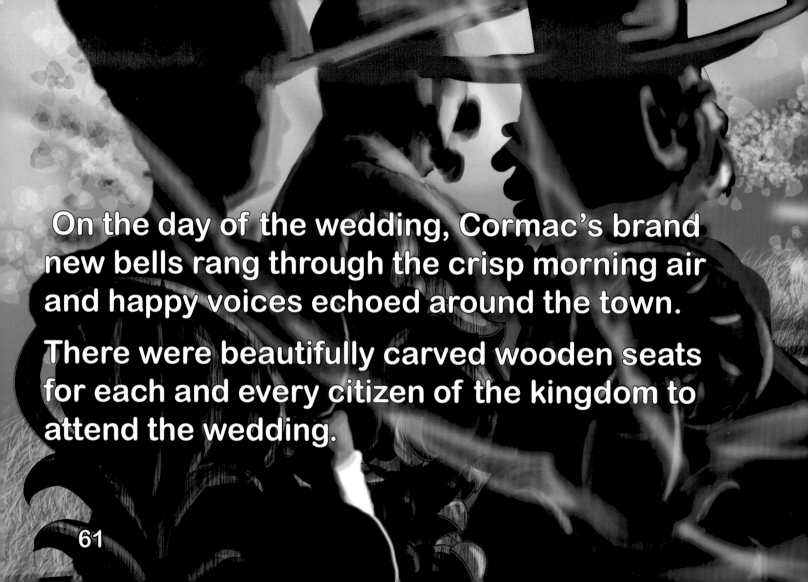

On the day of the wedding, Cormac's brand new bells rang through the crisp morning air and happy voices echoed around the town.

There were beautifully carved wooden seats for each and every citizen of the kingdom to attend the wedding.

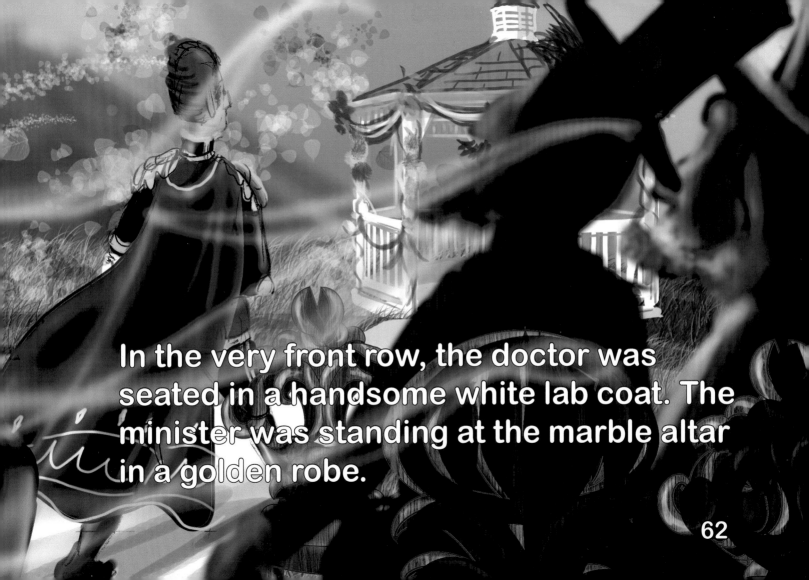

In the very front row, the doctor was seated in a handsome white lab coat. The minister was standing at the marble altar in a golden robe.

Georg, who had become the mayor of the town, walked Shana down the aisle. She wore a long white dress with a golden veil and a sparkling silver crown. And the prince, or now the king, I should say, was at the altar in a bright red jacket and a jet black tie with many medals of honor and bravery. He was beaming.

64

So it came to be that King James and Queen Shana were married. But the most amazing thing about this day was that the scar on King James's face had never really disappeared or changed at all. It was because he was so kind, that nobody ever noticed it anymore. Because it doesn't matter what you look like on the outside. It only matters what's on the inside.

67

And by this time, the Grouch's heart was so big that the Love Bug's new family could all fit inside. "Well," the Love Bug sighed, "this really turned out happily ever after."